This igloo book belongs to:

....

igloobooks

Published in 2019
by Igloo Books Ltd
Cottage Farm
Sywell
NN6 0BJ
www.igloobooks.com

Copyright © 2012 Igloo Books Ltd
Igloo Books is an imprint of Bonnier Books UK

GOL002 0519
12 14 16 15 13
ISBN: 978-0-85780-428-0

Printed and manufactured in China

Monkey Tricks

igloobooks

Little Monkey lives in the sprawly, crawly jungle.

He loves swinging by his tail and eating bananas. But Little Monkey is very cheeky. He likes to play tricks on some of his friends.

First, Snake hears Little Monkey calling for help.
"HELP! HELP!" he cries, jumping up and down.
"Little Monkey is in trouble!" cries Snake.

So Snake goes **HISS, HISSING** to the rescue.

But Little Monkey is playing a trick!
"BOO!" He leaps out of the hollow tree.
Snake jumps so much that she ties herself into a knot!

"Little Monkey, you're a pest!" hisses Snake, crossly.

"It's just a joke!" giggles Little Monkey.

Next, Little Lion hears Little Monkey's voice.

"HELP! HELP!" he cries, trying not to giggle.

"Little Monkey is in trouble!" cries Little Lion.

He goes **BOUND, BOUND, BOUNDING** to the rescue.

But Little Monkey is playing another trick!
Little Lion bounds into a pile of prickles.

"Little Monkey, you're a **nuisance!**" roars Little Lion.

"It's just a joke!" giggles Little Monkey.

Little Monkey plays tricks on **everyone**.

He creeps up on Little Crocodile. . .

. . . he frightens Little Armadillo. . .

...he even ties some twigs to Little Tiger's tail!

Little Monkey's friends meet by the long, yellow grass.
"I've had enough of Little Monkey's tricks," says Snake.

"I don't want to play with him any more," says Little Lion.
"It's not nice to play tricks," says Baby Hippo.

Then they hear Little Monkey's voice.

"HELP! HELP! I'M STUCK IN THE MUD!"

"He's playing tricks again!" says Little Crocodile.
"I'm not falling for his jokes anymore!"
says Little Armadillo.

But this time, Little Monkey really is in trouble!

Poor Little Monkey waits and waits for his friends.
But nobody comes.

"Why won't they help me?" Little Monkey sobs.
"How will I ever get out?"
Then he hears a voice.
"Little Monkey! Where are you?"

It's his mother!

She pulls Little Monkey out of the mud.

Then, she wipes his fur and washes him clean.
"None of my friends came to help me," sniffs Little Monkey, sadly.

"You play too many tricks," says his mother.
"They don't know when to believe you."

"What if they don't want to be my friends
anymore?" says Little Monkey.

"Don't be scared,"
says his mother, softly.
"They will be your friends
if you say you're sorry."

All of Little Monkey's friends gather around him.
"I'm sorry I played tricks on you," he says.
"Please will you forgive me and be my friends?"

"Of course, we will, Little Monkey!" they shout.
"We're your friends forever!"

But Little Monkey's friends have their own trick to play!

Baby Hippo jumps into the mud!
Little Monkey gets splashed.
"It's just a joke!" say his friends.

SPLOOSH!

"Goodbye!"